For my mother

www.enchantedlion.com

First English-language edition published in 2017 by Enchanted Lion Books
67 West Street, 317A, Brooklyn, NY 11222
Copyediting: Lawrence Kim, Kate Finney
Design & layout for the English-language edition: Lawrence Kim
Originally published in French as *Brindille* Copyright © Editions Milan, 2012
Book design for the French-language edition: Rémi Courgeon

ISBN 978-1-59270-210-7

Printed in China by R. R. Donnelley Asia Printing Solutions, Ltd.

First Printing

FEATHER

Rémi Courgeon

Translated from the French by Claudia Zoe Bedrick

ENCHANTED LION BOOKS

NEW YORK

Paulina.
Such a pretty name,
and yet everyone
called her Feather.
She lived with her dad
and three older brothers.
They weren't mean, exactly.
Just kind of rough and clumsy.
Feather was different.

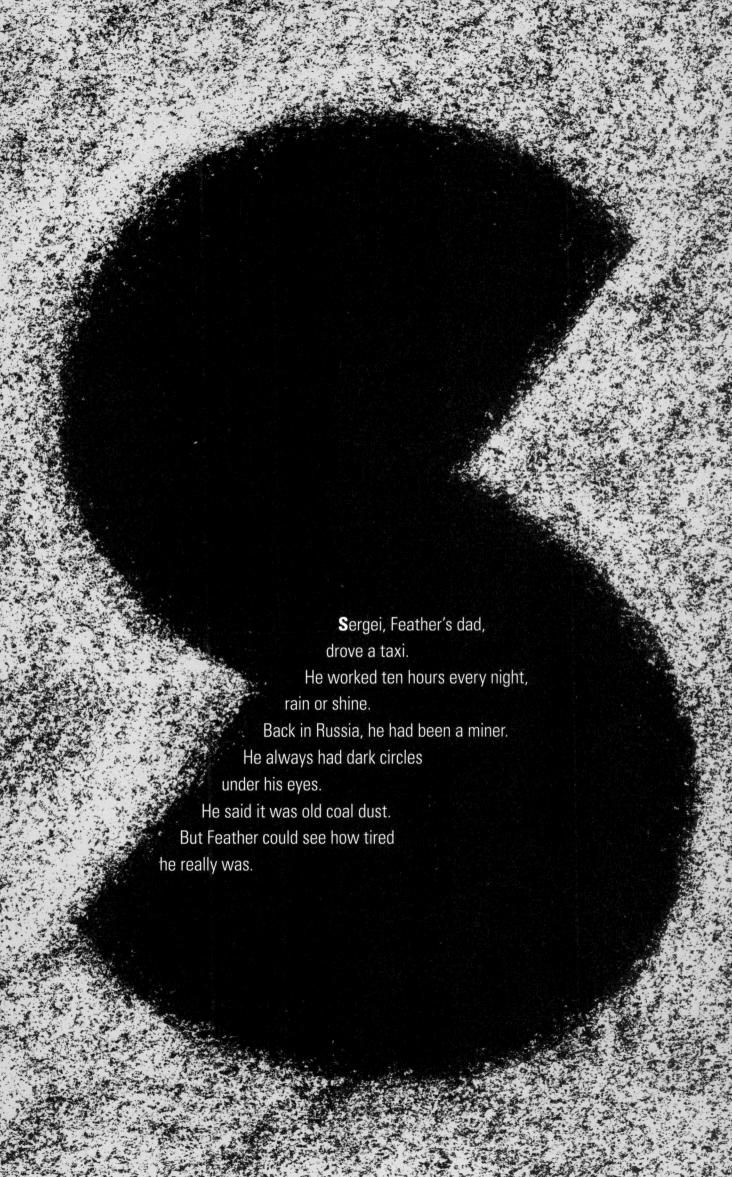

Sergei, Feather's dad,
drove a taxi.
He worked ten hours every night,
rain or shine.
Back in Russia, he had been a miner.
He always had dark circles
under his eyes.
He said it was old coal dust.
But Feather could see how tired
he really was.

Oleg,
the eldest brother,
thought, talked,
and breathed soccer.
Fortunately, at night
he only dreamed soccer,
so everyone could sleep.

Ivan,
the middle brother,
ate constantly.
Oleg nicknamed him "Blimp"
but Ivan got him back
by beating him up.

Vlad,
the youngest brother,
spent half his time on his bike
and the other half on his computer.
He didn't talk much.
Instead, he timed himself:
going to school,
doing math homework,
playing video games.

Feather was not only
the youngest of all
but also the smallest.

Though the only girl
in this family of boys,
Feather was far from spoiled.
They fought each other to decide
who would do the chores
and Feather usually lost.
So she ended up doing
the laundry and the ironing,
instead of what
she enjoyed the most:
playing the piano.

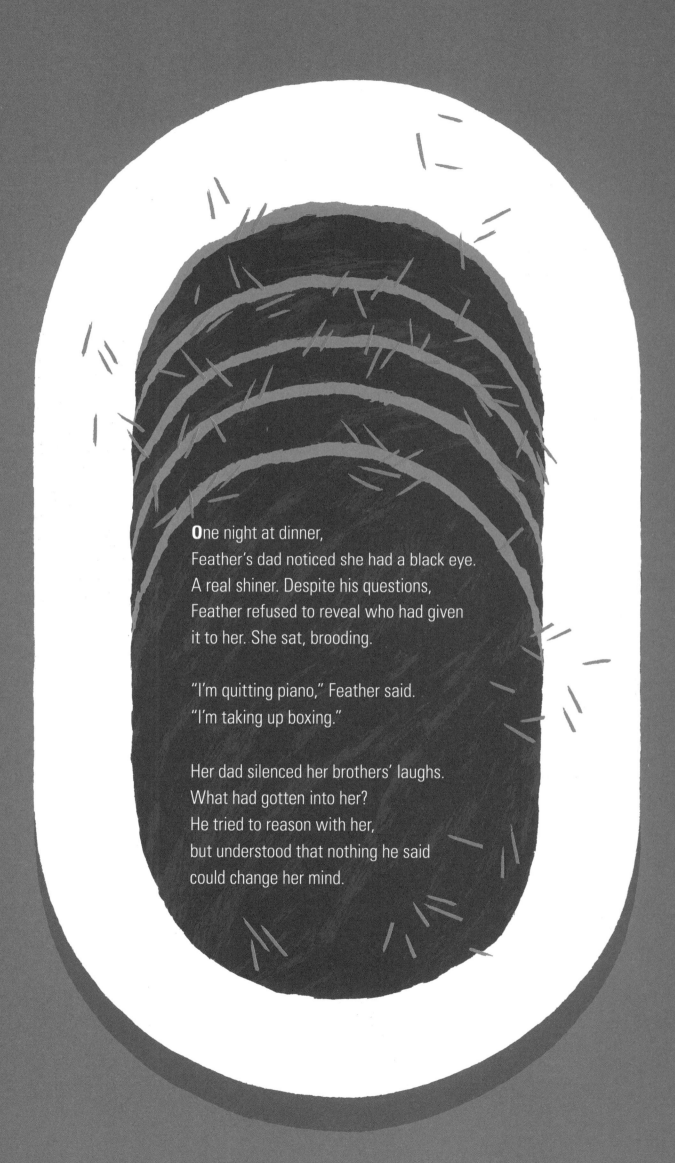

One night at dinner,
Feather's dad noticed she had a black eye.
A real shiner. Despite his questions,
Feather refused to reveal who had given
it to her. She sat, brooding.

"I'm quitting piano," Feather said.
"I'm taking up boxing."

Her dad silenced her brothers' laughs.
What had gotten into her?
He tried to reason with her,
but understood that nothing he said
could change her mind.

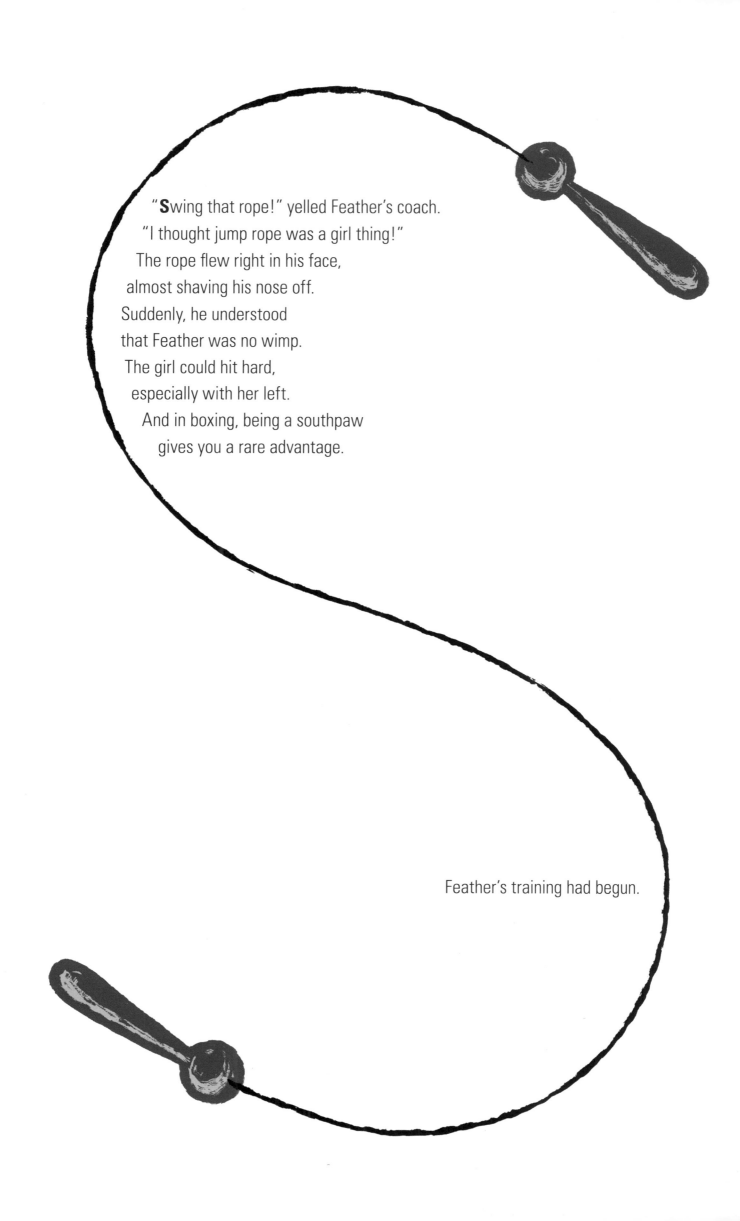

"**S**wing that rope!" yelled Feather's coach.
"I thought jump rope was a girl thing!"
The rope flew right in his face,
almost shaving his nose off.
Suddenly, he understood
that Feather was no wimp.
The girl could hit hard,
especially with her left.
And in boxing, being a southpaw
gives you a rare advantage.

Feather's training had begun.

In the weeks that followed,
Feather won more fights against
her brothers.

Which meant fewer chores.
And fewer chores meant more time to train.
And the more she trained, the more she beat her brothers.
Which meant even fewer chores.
Feather's killer left gave her confidence.
She even called Ivan "Blimp" once.
She had to run for it,
but running was part of her training, after all.

"**J**oin us, Feather,"
her dad said one night.
"Play us a little Mozart."
Feather sat down at the piano,
but when she put her fingers
on the keys and saw
how red and swollen they were,
she slammed the cover shut.
"Paulina!" she shouted.
"My name is Paulina!"
Then she stomped down the hall
to her room and slammed the door
behind her.

Wolfgang Amadeus Mozart, KV 423

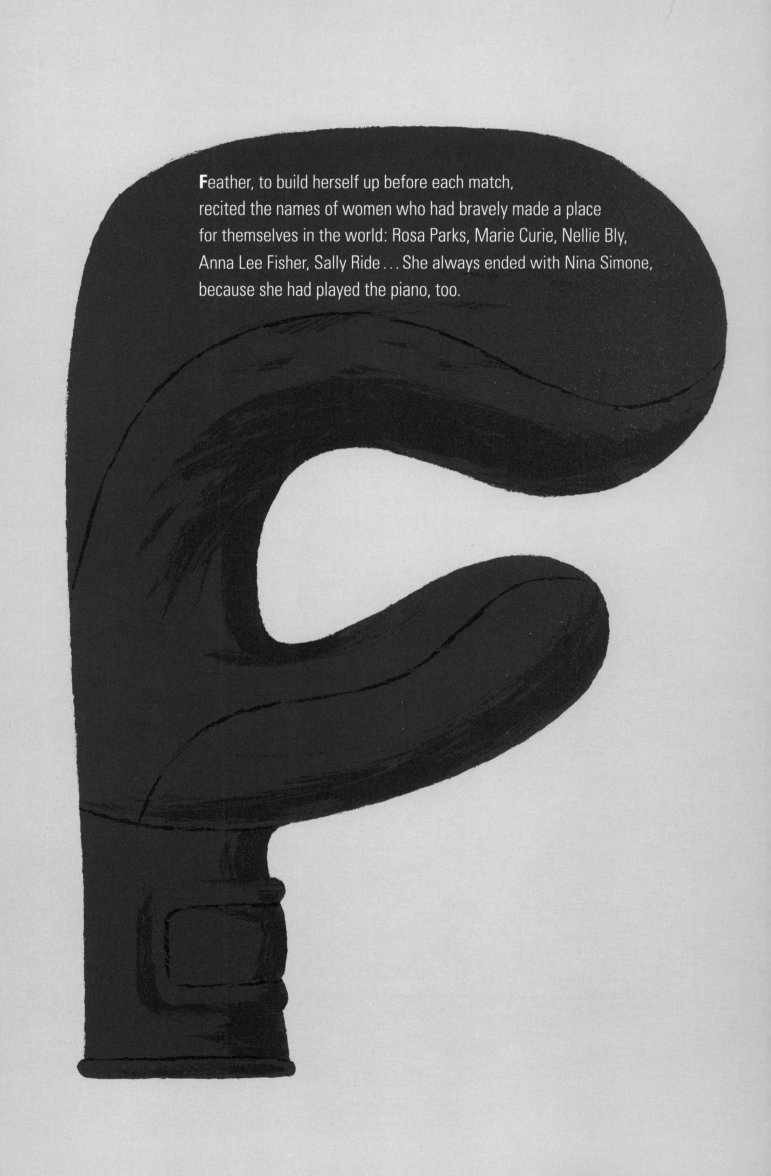

Feather, to build herself up before each match,
recited the names of women who had bravely made a place
for themselves in the world: Rosa Parks, Marie Curie, Nellie Bly,
Anna Lee Fisher, Sally Ride…She always ended with Nina Simone,
because she had played the piano, too.

"**L**et's go, let's go,"
warned her coach.
"The big fight's only a month away.
You've gotta be ready."
When Feather got home that night,
she didn't know
whether to laugh or cry.
Fear knotted her stomach.
A real match!
Her brothers shrugged at the news,
but they watched her with new attention.
Her dad asked,
"Are you really going to do this?"
But he already knew the answer.

The day before the match,
Feather decided not to train at all.
Instead, since the apartment
was empty, she calmed herself
by playing the piano.

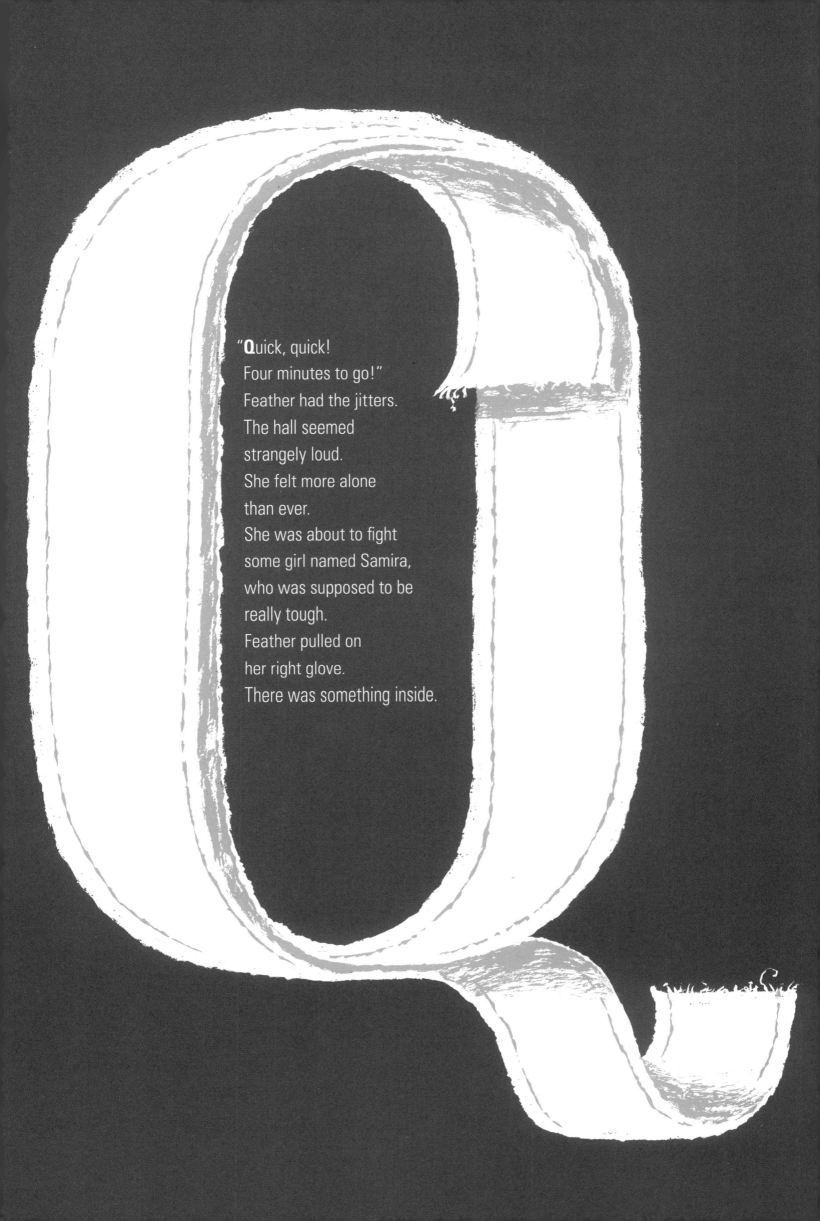

"**Q**uick, quick!
Four minutes to go!"
Feather had the jitters.
The hall seemed
strangely loud.
She felt more alone
than ever.
She was about to fight
some girl named Samira,
who was supposed to be
really tough.
Feather pulled on
her right glove.
There was something inside.

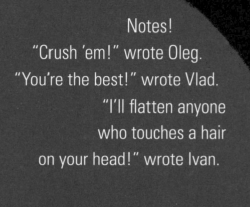

Notes!
"Crush 'em!" wrote Oleg.
"You're the best!" wrote Vlad.
"I'll flatten anyone
who touches a hair
on your head!" wrote Ivan.

Feather stuck the papers
back in her glove and put it on.
In her left glove, she found
a photograph of her mother.
The back read,
"We're with you, Paulina!
Love, Dad"

Paulina put everything she had into her left…

...and she won!

After Paulina's victory,
things began to change in her little family.
None of her brothers
became a master chef
or professional launderer,
but they all stopped calling her
Feather for good.
And the melodious sounds
of the piano filled their apartment
once more.

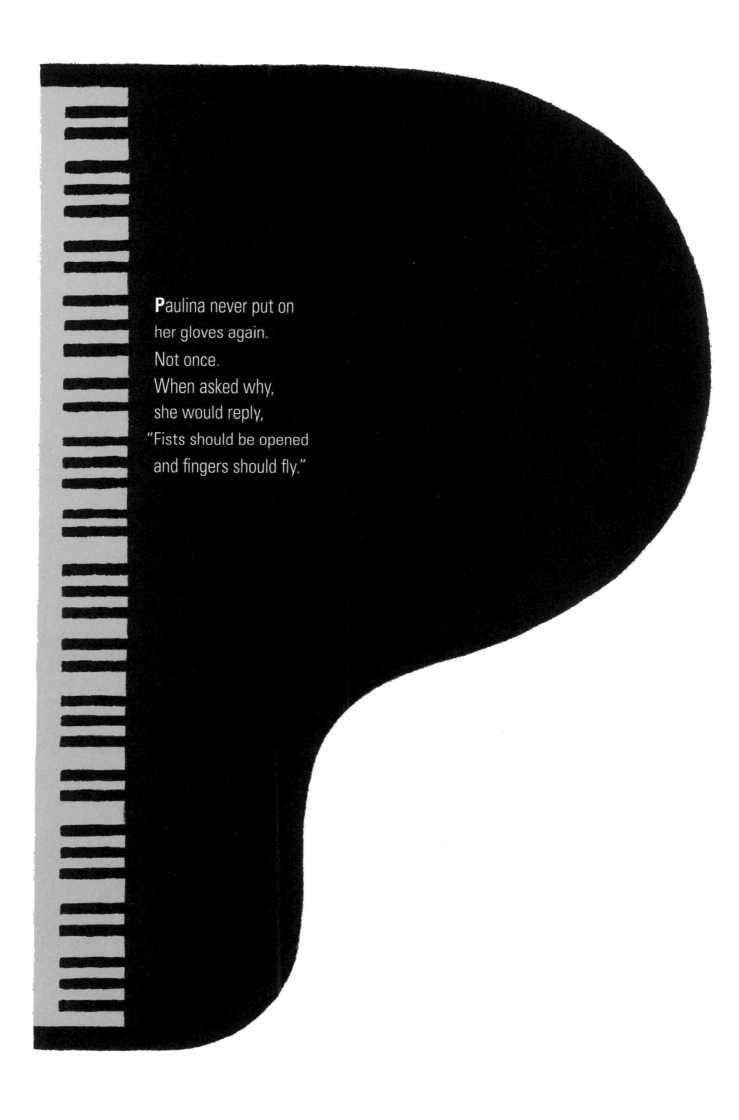

Paulina never put on
her gloves again.
Not once.
When asked why,
she would reply,
"Fists should be opened
and fingers should fly."